THE
BIG
PETER RABBIT
BOOK

THINGS TO DO • GAMES TO PLAY • STORIES
PRESENTS TO MAKE

From the original and authorized stories
BY BEATRIX POTTER

F. WARNE & Co.

FREDERICK WARNE
Penguin Books Ltd, Harmondsworth, Middlesex, England
Viking Penguin Inc., 40 West 23rd Street, New York, New York 10010, U.S.A.
Penguin Books Australia Ltd, Ringwood, Victoria, Australia
Penguin Books Canada Limited, 2801 John Street, Markham, Ontario, Canada L3R 1B4
Penguin Books (N.Z.) Ltd, 182-190 Wairau Road, Auckland 10, New Zealand

First published 1986

ISBN 0 7232 3409 4

This volume compiled by Sandy Ransford, Victorama Ltd, for Frederick Warne & Co. Designed by Clive Sutherland for Frederick Warne & Co.

Printed and bound in Great Britain by William Clowes Limited, Beccles and London

Contents

About Me 4
About Peter Rabbit 5
About Beatrix Potter 6
Beatrix Potter's Picture Letters 9
How to Paint Flowers 12
Code Writing 15
Peter Rabbit's Garden 16
Market Day 18
Robinson's Scavenger Hunt 19
A Puddle-Duck's Problem 20
A Puddle-Duck's Puzzle 22
Pond Life 24
Goodies to Make 26
Shopping Spree 28
For a Special Treat 30
Introducing Mrs. Tittlemouse 31

A Christmas Story 34
Needle Work 38
The Peter Rabbit Quiz 41
What's in a Name? 42
A Cat Tale 43
"Rabbit-Tobacco" 44
How to Make a Pop-up Card 46
Nature Notebook 48
Baking Day 50
Squirrel Nutkin's Riddles 52
Three Naughty Kittens 54
Peter Rabbit's Almanac 56
How to Give a Party 58
Peter Rabbit's Party 62
Answers to Puzzles 64

About Me

This is a page for you to fill in, very carefully, in your best handwriting. You could leave the last line to fill in until you have read all of this book.

MY SURNAME ....

MY FIRST NAME/S ....

MY BIRTHDAY ....

MY AGE .... YEARS .... MONTHS

MY ADDRESS ....

....

....

MY TELEPHONE NUMBER ....

THE PLACE WHERE I WAS BORN ....

....

MY SCHOOL ....

MY BROTHERS' AND SISTERS' NAMES ....

....

MY PETS ....

....

MY FAVOURITE BEATRIX POTTER CHARACTER ....

....

....

About Peter Rabbit

The Peter Rabbit of Beatrix Potter's stories was based on a live rabbit which she kept as a pet at her London home from 1892 to 1901. He was supposed to live in a hutch in the garden, but often came into the house, where he enjoyed lying in front of the fire, like a pet cat or dog.

Peter Rabbit, August 1899

In 1893 Beatrix Potter wrote and illustrated a letter containing a story about Peter, part of which is reproduced on pages 9, 10 and 11 of this book. It formed the basis of the first 'Peter Rabbit' book, which was first published in 1902.

Below is the story Peter's family tree, showing the names of his relations. We do not know about old Mrs. Benjamin Bunny, but either she or old Mr. Benjamin must have been related to Peter's parents, because Peter and Benjamin were cousins. It is fun to construct a family tree. Why not make one for your own family?

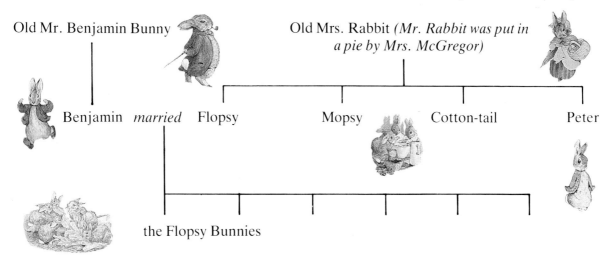

Old Mr. Benjamin Bunny

Old Mrs. Rabbit (*Mr. Rabbit was put in a pie by Mrs. McGregor*)

Benjamin *married* Flopsy   Mopsy   Cotton-tail   Peter

the Flopsy Bunnies

About Beatrix Potter

Helen Beatrix Potter was born on 28 July 1866. She lived at 2 Bolton Gardens, Earl's Court, a quiet area of London, where she spent much of her time alone. She was an only child until her brother Bertram was born five years later, and she did not go to school, but was taught at home by governesses.

Every spring and every summer the Potter family would go and stay in country houses—in Scotland, Wales, the Lake District, Hertfordshire—and here Beatrix and her brother used to escape from the dull, restricted life of London and delight in discovering the secrets of the countryside. They used to collect specimens of plants, insects and animals and take them home to study, producing drawings and paintings in little hand-sewn books.

As Beatrix grew older she became more and more absorbed in her painting and drawing. She still lived with her parents in London, though she much preferred the country, and kept pets in what had been the schoolroom—mice, bats, rabbits (firstly Benjamin Bunny, a tame Belgian rabbit, and later Peter, who was bought in west London for 4/6 [22½p]) and a hedgehog called Tiggy, who was the model for Mrs. Tiggy-winkle.

Beatrix Potter started to write her books in the late 1890s. The first *Tale of Peter Rabbit* had black and white drawings and was privately printed in 1901; a coloured edition was published a year later, and this was followed by *The Tale of Squirrel Nutkin* and *The Tailor of Gloucester* in 1903, and *The Tale of Benjamin Bunny* and *The Tale of Two Bad Mice* in 1904.

In 1905, partly from the money she had earned from her books, Beatrix Potter bought Hill Top Farm in the village of Sawrey in the Lake District.

A corner of the schoolroom at 2 Bolton Gardens, 26 November 1885

Mr. and Mrs. Potter, Beatrix and Bertram, July 1881

Beatrix Potter at fifteen

Mrs. Heelis (Beatrix Potter) discussing Herdwick tweed at the Woolpack Show, Eskdale

Beatrix Potter at Hill Top Farm, taken about 1907

(Hill Top is the farm pictured in *The Tale of Jemima Puddle-Duck,* and the inside of the house is shown in *The Tale of Samuel Whiskers.*) She never lived permanently in the house, being based in her parents' home in London, but she spent as much time there as she could, overseeing the running of the farm.

It was during the years from 1905 to 1913, when she married William Heelis, a Lake District solicitor, that Beatrix Potter wrote most of her books. After her marriage she lived at Castle Cottage, on another farm next to Hill Top, and devoted her life to

Mrs. Tabitha Twitchit searching for her son, Thomas. This picture from The Tale of Samuel Whiskers *shows the landing at Hill Top Farm.*

farming. She became a highly respected sheep farmer and when she died, aged seventy-seven, on 22 December 1943, she left 4000 acres to the National Trust. She requested that the rooms at Hill Top be left as they were when she used them, and visitors today can see the house as it was, and recognise the scenes shown in her books.

A photograph of the landing at Hill Top Farm

Beatrix Potter's Picture Letters

The story of Peter Rabbit was first told in an illustrated letter sent by Beatrix Potter to the five-year-old son of her former governess and companion, when he was ill. The little boy was called Noel Moore, and he lived in Wandsworth, in south-west London. The letter was written on 4 September 1893, and was sent from Eastwood House, Dunkeld, Perthshire in Scotland, where Beatrix Potter was on holiday. Fortunately Noel kept it, and when, a few years later, Beatrix Potter had the idea of turning the story into a little book she borrowed the letter from him. *The Tale of Peter Rabbit* is based upon it.

Below is a reproduction of the first page of the letter, with the first page of *Peter Rabbit* to compare it with. On the following two pages the original drawings from the letter are reproduced but the text has been printed to make it easier to read.

ONCE upon a time there were four little Rabbits, and their names were —

Flopsy,

Mopsy,

Cotton-tail,

and Peter.

They lived with their Mother in a sand-bank, underneath the root of a very big fir-tree.

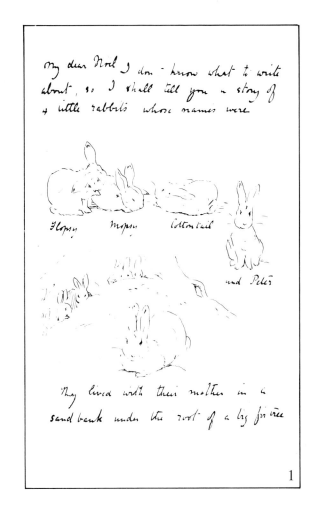

"Now, my dears," said old Mrs. Bunny, "you may go into the field or down the lane, but don't go into Mr. McGregor's garden."

Flopsy, Mopsy and Cottontail, who were good little rabbits, went down the lane to gather blackberries, but Peter,

2

who was very naughty, ran straight away to Mr. McGregor's garden and squeezed underneath the gate.
First he ate some lettuce, and some broad beans, then some radishes, and then, feeling rather sick, he went to look for some parsley; but round the end of the cucumber frame whom should he meet but Mr. McGregor!

3

Mr. McGregor was planting out young cabbages but he jumped up and ran after Peter waving a rake and calling out "Stop thief!"

Peter was most dreadfully frightened and rushed all over the garden, for he had forgotten the way back to the gate.

4

He lost one of his shoes among the cabbages and the other shoe amongst the potatoes. After losing them he ran on four legs and went faster, so that I think he would have got away altogether, if he had not unfortunately run into a gooseberry net and got caught fast by the large buttons on his jacket. It was a blue jacket with brass buttons, quite new.

Mr. McGregor came up with a basket which he intended to pop on top of   5

Peter, but Peter wriggled out just in time, leaving his jacket behind, and this time he found the gate, slipped underneath and ran home safely.

Mr. McGregor hung up the little jacket and shoes for a scarecrow, to frighten the blackbirds.   6

Peter was ill during the evening, in consequence of overeating himself. His mother put him to bed and gave him a dose of camomile tea, but Flopsy,

Mopsy, and Cottontail had bread and milk and blackberries for supper.

7

How to Paint Flowers

As well as being a writer and illustrator of children's books, Beatrix Potter was known as a painter of flowers, plants and wildlife. When she was young children were taught to paint by their teachers and governesses. Although you may think that only a few talented people are able to paint, in years gone by this teaching showed that most people could produce a painting of some kind if they tried, and it is the same today.

The first thing to learn is how to look at the subject of your painting. Study it carefully and see what is really there. For example, if you were going to paint a picture of your garden, you might think that a flat green area would depict the lawn, but if you really study a lawn you will see that it is made up of lots of different shades of green, and probably has some yellowy or browny bits in it too. Nothing is ever a flat colour, because light falls on part of it, making it brighter, while another part of it will be in shadow, making it darker.

The second thing to remember is that most paintings have to be built up, stage by stage, from sketches. Look at the two pictures below and you will see how Beatrix Potter built up some of her pictures.

So if you want to paint a flower, pick one from the garden, bring it into the house, and look at it. Choose an

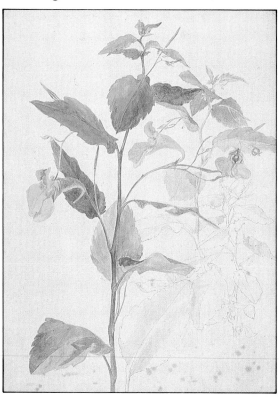

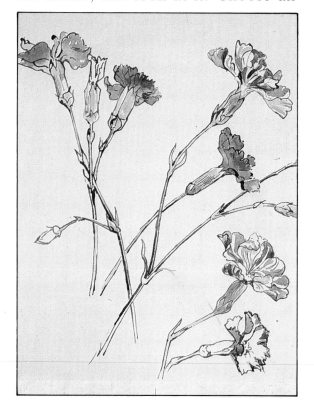

Above: *From Beatrix Potter's drawing book when she was ten*

easy flower like a buttercup. Flowers with lots of petal, like roses, are very difficult to draw and paint. Put your flower where you can look right into its face, and study it for a few moments. Notice where the light and the shadows fall, and any markings on the petals. When you think you know your flower, try drawing it lightly in pencil first to work out its shape.

Below: *Bramble leaves painted by Beatrix Potter when she was fourteen*

When the time comes to paint, make sure that your paints, brushes and water are all clean. You cannot get true, clear colours if they are not. If the water gets dirty as you paint, then change it.

Moisten your brush in the water, then wipe it on the paint. Don't make it too wet or you will have trouble controlling it. Paint the lighter parts of the flower first, then add a touch of a darker colour to paint the shadowed areas. Again, you must be very careful not to have the paint too wet or the colours will run together and make a nasty muddy mess.

If you find you can paint a single flower quite easily, try adding its stalk and leaves, and then try to paint several flowers together in a vase. If you are not very good at it, don't be disheartened. Keep practising and one day you will find that it becomes much easier.

Once you can paint flowers, you can use your skill to help decorate all kinds of things; for example, the invitations on page 30, the pop-up card on pages 46 and 47, and letters to friends. Your parents will probably be pleased to receive something painted by you, too.

These flowers were drawn when Beatrix Potter was nine.

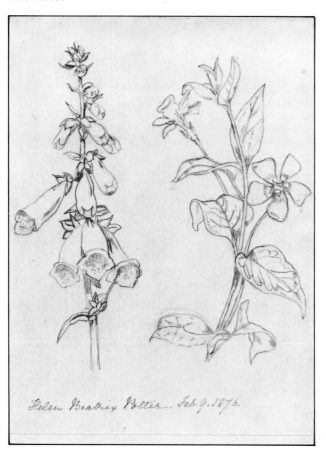

Foxglove and periwinkle, 9 February 1876

Narcissus, March 1876

Code Writing

Between the ages of fifteen and thirty Beatrix Potter kept a journal, or diary, written in a code that she had made up herself and which no one else could read. It was not until fifteen years after her death that the key to the code was discovered, and the journal took another six years to de-code!

Here is Beatrix Potter's code alphabet. As you can see, some letters are almost the same as real ones, and some are very different.

The Code Alphabet					
a	a	ꜧ	k	ʊ	u
ʟ	b	t	l	ɳ	v
ꝛ	c	n	m	ʍ	w
ơ	d	m	n	x	x
k	e	e	o	ꝲ	y
c	f	Ꝓ	p	ꝛ	z
ơ	g	q	q	2	to, too, two
ʟ	h	ꙍ	r	3	the, three
ʟ	i	ꝩ	s	4	for, four
ʟ	j	1	t	+	and

A	B	C	D	E	F	G	H	I
Z	Y	X	W	V	U	T	S	R
J	K	L	M	N	O	P	Q	R
Q	P	O	N	M	L	K	J	I
S	T	U	V	W	X	Y	Z	
H	G	F	E	D	C	B	A	

You could make up a cipher of your own and write secret messages in it, but meanwhile see if you can decipher the following messages. One uses Beatrix Potter's cipher, the others use the examples above.

ʟ k a 1 ꙍ ʟ x   ꝩ e 1 1 k ꙍ

ʟ a ơ a 1 a n k   ꙍ a ʟ ʟ ʟ 1

ꝛ a t t k ơ   ꝩ k 1 k ꙍ

16 5 20 5 18 19
3 15 21 19 9 14
2 5 14 10 1 13 9 14
13 1 18 18 9 5 4
6 12 15 16 19 25
16 5 20 5 18 19   19 9 19 20 5 18

K V G V I D Z H Z
M Z F T S G B
I Z Y Y R G D S L
W R H L Y V B V W
S R H N L G S V I

Strictly speaking it is not a code at all, but a *cipher*. A code is a system in which one letter, number or word can stand for a complete message. For example, 'X' or '10' or 'Brighton' might mean 'the package has been delivered'. With a cipher, each letter of the alphabet is replaced by another letter, number or symbol. Here are two simple cipher alphabets:

A	B	C	D	E	F	G	H	I
1	2	3	4	5	6	7	8	9
J	K	L	M	N	O	P	Q	R
10	11	12	13	14	15	16	17	18
S	T	U	V	W	X	Y	Z	
19	20	21	22	23	24	25	26	

Peter Rabbit's Garden

When Peter Rabbit grew up he kept a market garden, in which he grew delicious vegetables to eat. Some vegetables, like radishes, can be grown very quickly and easily in a garden, and others, like mustard and cress, can be grown in pots on a windowsill. Here's how to create your own small vegetable garden, just like Peter Rabbit's.

a couple of weeks, if the little plants look crowded together, thin them out to about 6 cm (2½ in) apart. This means removing the weaker looking plants and leaving the strong ones to grow sturdy. Keep the young plants well watered, and in about five weeks they should be ready for eating. Pull them up and you will see the radish just under the surface of the soil.

Radishes

Radishes are a salad vegetable and need to be grown outdoors. Buy a packet of seeds and decide where in the garden you will plant them. Then, with the help of an adult, make sure the soil has been dug over and raked smooth before you plant the seeds.

Sow the seeds in spring in rows about 1 cm (½ in) deep and 3 cm (1¼ in) apart. Water the ground when you have planted them, and then check them every day. When the earth becomes dry, water them again. After a few days you will see little green leaves appearing out of the soil. After

Parsley

Peter Rabbit went looking for parsley when he had eaten too much in Mr.

McGregor's garden. It is a delicious herb, which you can eat in a salad, chop up and sprinkle over new potatoes, or use in a sauce. It can be grown out in the garden or indoors in a pot.

Plant the seeds about 1 cm (½ in) deep in the soil outside or in a pot and keep them watered. Sometimes they take several weeks to come up, but when they do they will grow quite quickly. Let the plant grow until it is 6 cm (2½ in) or so tall, then cut the leaves off with scissors as you want to use them.

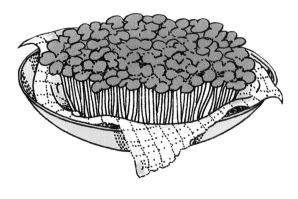

Mustard and Cress

Mustard and cress can be grown in pots of soil, like the parsley, or in a saucer lined with damp paper towels. Whichever you do, sow the cress seeds first and the mustard seeds three or four days later, so that they will come up at the same time. Keep the pot or saucer in a warm place such as on a kitchen windowsill, cover it to keep out the light and keep it watered. When the little plants are about 2 cm (1 in) high, remove the cover and let them grow for about another ten days until they are 4 - 5 cm high (2 in) when

they will be ready for cutting and eating.

Carrot Tops

If you want to grow some pretty, feathery leaves for a rabbit to eat, cut the tops off some carrots and put them with the cut side down on a saucer filled with 2 cm (1 in) of water. Put the dish on a windowsill and keep the water level up by adding water each day. After a few days the leaves will start to grow. They make pretty decorations as well as good rabbit food.

MARKET DAY

and cauliflowers, and to buy tea, blue bag, soap, darning-wool, yeast and cabbage seed. It was a long walk, and there were many narrow stiles to climb through.

Little pig Robinson lived in Devonshire, with his aunts, Miss Dorcas and Miss Porcas, at a farm called Piggery Porcombe. Their cosy thatched cottage was in an orchard at the top of a steep red Devonshire lane.

Aunt Dorcas was a stout speckled pig who kept hens. Aunt Porcas was a large smiling black pig who took in washing.

The aunts sent Robinson to market in Stymouth, to sell their eggs, daffodils

The market hall was a large, airy, light, cheerful, covered-in place. There was a loud hum of voices; market folk cried their wares; customers elbowed and pushed round the stalls.

Robinson found a standing place at one end of a stall where Nanny Nettigoat was selling periwinkles. He stood on an empty box quite proud and bold behind the trestle table, singing:

"Eggs, new laid! Fresh new-laid eggs! Who'll come and buy my eggs and daffodillies?"

And in a very short time he had sold all his produce, and was able to go and buy six sticks of delightfully sticky barley sugar with the pennies he had earned.

From *The Tale of Little Pig Robinson*

18

Robinson's Scavenger Hunt

Pigs like Robinson are great scavengers, because they eat all kinds of waste food like potato peelings that people and other animals do not want. To scavenge means to collect and carry away things that other people do not want, and a scavenger hunt is a game in which you try and collect all the items given in a list.

Below is a list of items that you should be able to find quite easily around the house and garden, though one or two of them may be more difficult. See how quickly you can find them all, and award yourself the points given for each item. You can play the game on your own or with a friend, and if you play with a friend you can see who gets the better score. If you find it impossible to collect all the things in one day, allow yourself a week-end, or a week in the holidays, in which to find them all.

	Points
1. A used stamp.	4
2. A skipping rope.	2
3. A stone with a hole through it.	10
4. A forked twig.	2
5. A lump of sugar.	4
6. Something written in a foreign language.	8
7. A bird's feather.	5
8. A piece of play doh.	2
9. A bag with a shop's name on it.	1
10. A holiday brochure.	7
11. An apple.	1
12. A bus or railway timetable.	9
13. A blue flower (in spring or summer) OR An acorn in its cup (in autumn or winter).	5
14. A piece of white string.	4
15. An envelope with the address typed on it.	2
16. A newspaper from last week.	3
17. An empty sweet wrapper.	1
18. A Christmas decoration.	6
19. A yellow pencil.	3
20. A coin dated 1985.	5

A Puddle-Duck's Problem

What a funny sight it is to see a brood of ducklings with a hen!—Listen to the story of Jemima Puddle-duck, who was annoyed because the farmer's wife would not let her hatch her own eggs.

She tried to hide her eggs; but they were always found and carried off.

Jemima Puddle-duck became quite desperate. She determined to make a nest right away from the farm.

She set off on a fine spring afternoon along the cart-road that leads over the hill.

She was wearing a shawl and a poke bonnet.

When she reached the top of the hill, she saw a wood in the distance.

She thought that it looked a safe quiet spot.

Jemima began to waddle about in search of a convenient dry nesting-place. She rather fancied a tree-stump amongst some tall fox-gloves.

But—seated upon the stump, she was startled to find an elegantly dressed gentleman reading a news-paper.

He had black prick ears and sandy coloured whiskers.

"Madam, have you lost your way?" said he.

Jemima thought him mighty civil and handsome. She explained that she had not lost her way, but that she was trying to find a convenient dry nesting-place.

"Ah! is that so? indeed!" said the gentleman with the sandy whiskers, looking curiously at Jemima. "I have a sackful of feathers in my woodshed. You may sit there as long as you like."

He led the way to a very retired, dismal-looking house amongst the fox-gloves.

There was a tumble-down shed at the back of the house, made of old soap-boxes. The gentleman opened the door, and showed Jemima in.

The shed was almost quite full of feathers—it was almost suffocating; but it was comfortable and very soft.

Jemima Puddle-duck was rather surprised to find such a vast quantity of feathers. But it was very comfort-able; and she made a nest without any trouble at all.

From *The Tale of Jemima Puddle-Duck*

21

A Puddle-Duck's Puzzle

Jemima lays her eggs in the shed belonging to the sandy-whiskered gentleman. But the shed is so full of feathers that it is quite difficult to find the way through them to the eggs. Can you trace the path that Jemima has to follow to reach her eggs?

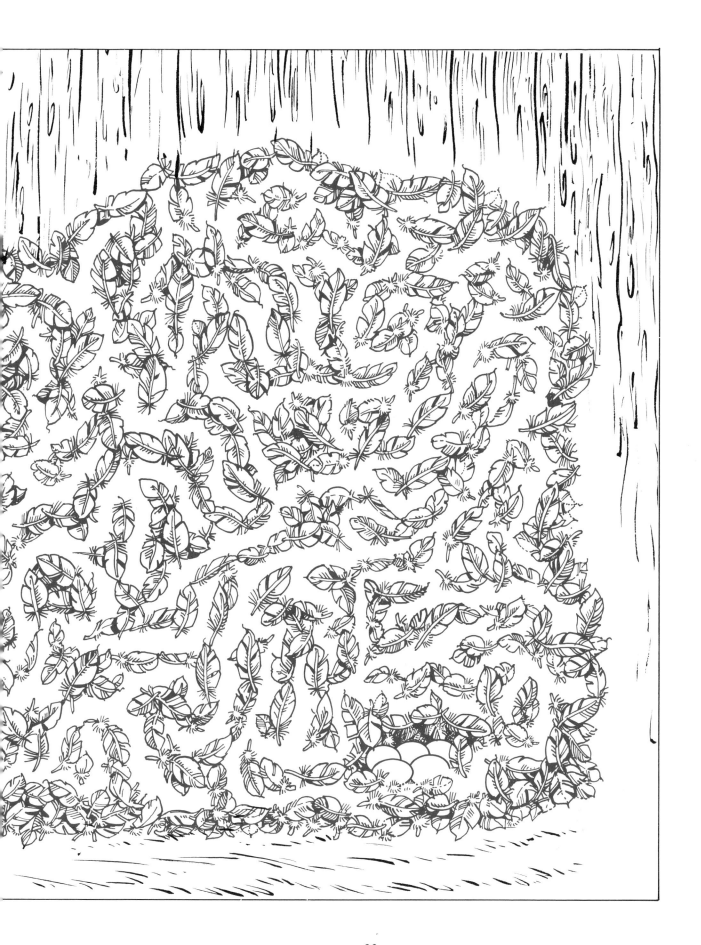

Pond Life

frogspawn   *tadpoles*   *baby frog*

Mr. Jeremy Fisher lived in a little damp house amongst the buttercups at the edge of a pond.

If you look at a pond in spring you may see clumps of transparent jelly with black spots in them near the pond's edge. This is frogspawn—the eggs from which frogs develop. The eggs hatch into tadpoles at first, but they gradually grow legs and lose their tails to become tiny frogs.

Some insects found around ponds can walk on the water. This is because the surface of the water forms a fine 'skin' which supports them. You may see water spiders, water boatmen and pond skaters doing this.

water spider   *water boatman*   *duckweed*   *pond skater*

24

Mr. Jeremy Fisher went fishing in a boat that looked like a lily leaf.

These plants are water lilies. The small-leaved green plant which sometimes covers the surface of ponds is called duckweed. You can see a picture of it on the opposite page.

When you next visit a pond, wait quietly at the edge for a while and then look down into the water. Be careful not to fall in! You may see a stickleback, a small fish about 5cm long with three spines sticking up from its back, like the one in the picture.

In the late afternoon or early evening of a calm day in summer you may suddenly hear a "plop" as a fish jumps, and see the widening ripples that form on the water where it lands. Keep still and quiet and watch very carefully and you will see the fish, too.

Goodies to Make

The sweets and candies on these pages are fun to make (and to eat!) at any time, but they are especially good as party presents. Wrap them separately in pieces of cling film and then put several of them on a piece of pretty wrapping paper, fold it round, and twist it at one end to make a little bag. Secure it with a piece of ribbon or a coloured rubber band.

Conversation Peppermints

Ingredients
275g (2 cups) icing or
   confectioners' sugar
1 egg white
1 teaspoon peppermint
   essence/extract

1. Sieve the sugar into a bowl.
2. Ask an adult to separate the egg white from the yolk and to put the white in a large bowl. Whisk it with a fork until it becomes frothy.
3. Stir the sugar into the egg white a little at a time until it is all mixed together.
4. Add the peppermint essence/extract and mix well.
5. Knead the mixture into a soft ball then divide it into small pieces. Roll these into little balls then pat them flat with your hands.
6. Put the mints on a sheet of greaseproof or waxed paper. After about half an hour, use the pointed end of a skewer to write a letter of the alphabet on each. Leave out Q, X, Y and Z.
7. Leave the mints overnight to harden.

Orange Fondants

Ingredients
grated rind of 1 orange
2 tablespoons orange juice
2 tablespoons lemon juice
350g (2½ cups) icing or
   confectioners' sugar
1 egg white
orange food colouring
angelica or candied peel

1. Ask an adult to grate the rind off the orange and to separate the egg yolk and white.
2. Sieve the sugar into a bowl.
3. Whisk the egg white.
4. Mix the orange rind and orange and lemon juices together and stir them into the sugar.
5. Stir the egg white into the mixture.
6. Add a few drops of orange colouring.
7. Knead the mixture and shape it into a number of small balls.
8. Rub the balls lightly on the grater to give them an orange skin appearance, then add a small piece of angelica or candied peel to each for the stalk.

9. Put the fondants on a sheet of greaseproof or waxed paper and leave overnight to harden.

Coconut Ice

Ingredients
250g (2 cups) icing or
  confectioners' sugar
175g (2 cups) desiccated or
  shredded coconut
small tin of condensed milk
pink food colouring

1. Ask an adult to open the tin of condensed milk and pour it into a mixing bowl.
2. Sieve the sugar into the bowl and mix it with the condensed milk.
3. Add the coconut and stir that in too. The mixture should feel stiff.
4. Divide the mixture into two halves. To one half add a few drops of pink food colouring and knead the mixture until it is an even pink colour.
5. Shape the white mixture and the pink mixture into two flattish bars and place one above the other. Press them together and leave them until they are firm.
6. Cut the bars into squares. One half of each square will be pink, and one half will be white.

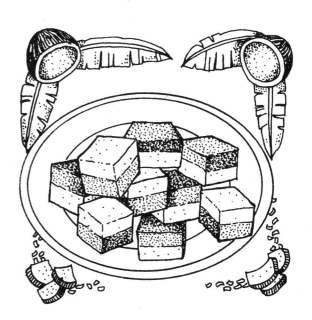

27

Shopping Spree

On this page and the one opposite is a game to play called an observation test. The two pictures show Ginger and Pickles's shop. It is a little village shop with a counter at a convenient height for rabbits, and it is kept by Ginger, a yellow tom-cat, and Pickles, a terrier. You can see them behind the counter in the picture on the opposite page. Underneath each picture are questions printed upside down. The idea is to study each picture for one minute (time yourself with a watch or ask someone else to time you) and then turn the book upside down and see if you can answer all the questions about it. It's a good game to play with a friend, to see who can answer the most questions correctly. The answers are given on page 64, but don't give up too soon!

1. What are the squirrels doing?
2. What kind of baby birds are in the picture?
3. What colour bonnet is the duck wearing?
4. Who appears on the left-hand side of the picture?
5. What can you read in the picture?

1. How many rabbits are in the picture?

2. Who is waiting to be served?

3. If you face the counter looking at the shop-keepers, as the customer is doing, is Ginger on the the right, or Pickles?

4. Who is taking his shoes off?

5. One animal appears in both pictures. Who?

6. How many animals are wearing green?

7. How many animals are wearing red?

For a Special Treat

When Ribby the cat asked Duchess the dog to tea she sent her an *invitation*.

When you want to invite a friend to tea, or a number of friends to a party, you need to send them invitations. Here is one addressed to Mr. Jeremy Fisher.

Mr. Jeremy Fisher,
Pond House.

Mr. Alderman
Ptolemy Tortoise
Requests the pleasure of
Mr. Jeremy Fisher's
Company at Dinner
on Dec. 25th
(there will be a snail)
R. S. V. P.

And here is his acceptance of it.

Mr Alderman Ptolemy Tortoise,
Melon Pit,
South Border.

Mr. Jeremy Fisher accepts with
pleasure Alderman P. Tortoise's
kind invitation to dinner for
Dec. 25.

A more modern version, which you could send to your friends, would be:

Dear .... (your friend's name)

Come to a party!

I am having a party on

.... (the date of the party)
(your address)

at ....

....

from .... *until* .... (the time of the party)

I do hope you can come!

Lots of love,

.... (your name)

R.S.V.P.

R. S. V. P. stands for *Répondez S'il Vous Plaît*, which is French for 'please reply'.

Write your invitations on coloured cards, and draw little pictures on them to make them look pretty.

Introducing Mrs. Tittlemouse

Mrs. Thomasina Tittlemouse is a little wood-mouse who lives in a house in a bank under a hedge. It has many sandy-floored passages leading to storerooms and nut-cellars and seed-cellars, and Mrs. Tittlemouse is very particular to keep it clean and tidy. She is forever shooing out creepy-crawlies because of the mess they make with their many feet, and she especially dislikes visits from Mr. Jackson, the toad, because he never wipes his very wet feet.

On the next two pages is a game based on *The Tale of Mrs. Tittlemouse*, for between two and four players. Open the book out flat and use the pages as a board. You will need a die and something to shake it in, and each player will also need a 'man' to mark his or her place on the board. Below are some that you can make for yourself. Trace the drawings on to a piece of card, colour them with crayons, then cut them out and fold them along the dotted line so that they will stand up. If you do not want to make the 'men', then ordinary coloured counters may be used instead.

You have to throw a 6 before you can start, and the aim of the game is to reach the party on square 24 before the other players do.

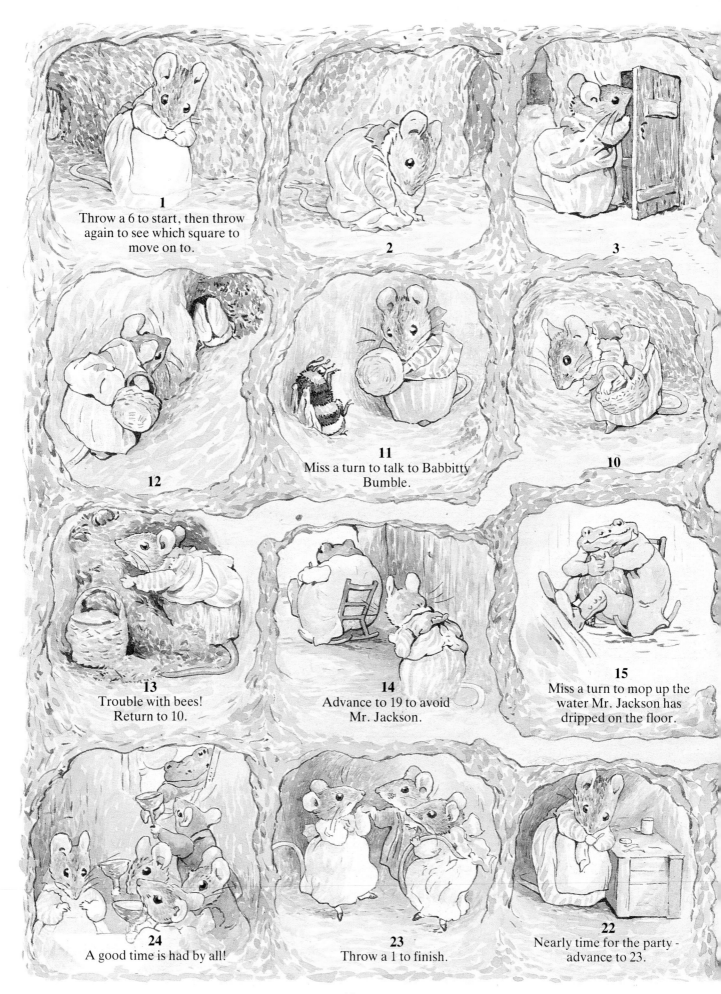

1
Throw a 6 to start, then throw again to see which square to move on to.

2

3

12

11
Miss a turn to talk to Babbitty Bumble.

10

13
Trouble with bees! Return to 10.

14
Advance to 19 to avoid Mr. Jackson.

15
Miss a turn to mop up the water Mr. Jackson has dripped on the floor.

24
A good time is had by all!

23
Throw a 1 to finish.

22
Nearly time for the party - advance to 23.

4
Miss a turn to shoo away the beetle.

5

6
Return to 2 to show the ladybird the way out.

9
Success! Advance to 12.

8
A large spider is sheltering from the rain. Throw a 6 to get rid of him and then throw again to move on.

7

16
Mr. Jackson has no teeth to eat the dinner he's offered - return to 3 to check the stores.

17
Off in search of honey - advance to 19.

18
Creepy-crawlies! Return to 12.

21

20
Mr. Jackson meets Babbitty Bumble - return to 15.

19

A Christmas Story

Some 300 years ago, when gentlemen carried swords and wore long wigs and full-skirted coats, a poor tailor was making a splendid coat of cherry-coloured corded silk and a cream-coloured satin waistcoat for the Mayor of Gloucester.

It was a few days before Christmas and very cold. The tailor worked all day and by the time it got dark all the silk and satin lay cut out on the table, ready to sew together in the morning. All that was missing was one single skein of cherry-coloured twisted silk.

The tailor came out of his shop at dark, for he did not sleep there at nights; he fastened the window and locked the door, and took away the key. No one lived there at night but little brown mice, and they run in and out without any keys!

He shuffled off through the snow to his home in College Court where he lived with his cat, Simpkin. The tailor was tired, so, taking his last four pennies, he sent Simpkin out to buy provisions—and a skein of cherry-coloured silk.

While the cat was out the tailor discovered little mice trapped under tea-cups and bowls on the dresser, and let them go free. But when Simpkin returned he was angry with the tailor, for he had been looking forward to a supper of fat mouse, so he hid the skein of silk in the tea-pot. It was a mean thing to do, for the tailor was beginning to be ill with a fever.

All that day he was ill, and the next day, and the next; and what should become of the cherry-coloured coat? In the tailor's shop in Westgate Street the embroidered silk and satin lay cut out upon the table—one-and-twenty button-holes—and who should come to sew them, when the window was barred, and the door was fast locked?

The tailor lay ill for three days and nights; and then it was Christmas Eve, and very late at night. The moon climbed up over the roofs and chimneys, and looked down over the gateway into College Court. There were no lights in the windows, nor any sound in the houses; all the city of Gloucester was fast asleep under the snow.

Simpkin still wanted his mice. When the Cathedral clock struck twelve he heard it, and came out of the tailor's door and wandered about in the snow.

From the tailor's shop in Westgate came a glow of light; and when Simpkin crept up to peep in at the window it was full of candles. There was a snippeting of scissors, and snappeting of thread; and little mouse voices sang loudly and gaily—

"Four-and-twenty tailors
Went out to catch a snail,
The best man amongst them
Durst not touch her tail;
She put out her horns
Like a little kyloe cow,
Run, tailors, run! or she'll have you all e'en now!"

"Mew! Mew!" interrupted Simpkin, and he scratched at the door. But the key was under the tailor's pillow, he could not get in.

"Mew! scratch! scratch!" scuffled Simpkin on the window-sill; while the little mice inside sprang to their feet, and all began to shout at once in little twittering voices: "No more twist! No more twist!" And they barred up the window shutters and shut out Simpkin.

Simpkin came away from the shop and went home, considering in his mind. He found the poor old tailor without fever, sleeping peacefully.

Then Simpkin went out on tip-toe and took a little parcel of silk out of the tea-pot, and looked at it in the moonlight; and he felt quite ashamed of his badness compared with those good little mice!

When the tailor awoke in the morning, the first thing which he saw upon the patchwork quilt, was a skein of cherry-coloured twisted silk, and beside the bed stood the repentant Simpkin!

"Alack, I am worn to a ravelling," said the Tailor of Gloucester, "but I have my twist!"

The sun was shining on the snow when the tailor got up and dressed, and came out into the street with Simpkin running before him.

"Alack," said the tailor, "I have my twist; but no more strength—nor time—than will serve to make me one single button-hole; for this is Christmas Day in the Morning! The Mayor of Gloucester shall be married by noon—and where is his cherry-coloured coat?"

He unlocked the door of the little shop in Westgate Street, and Simpkin ran in, like a cat that expects something.

But there was no one there! Not even one little brown mouse!

The boards were swept clean; the little ends of thread and the little silk snippets were all tidied away, and gone from the floor.

But upon the table—oh joy! the tailor gave a shout—there, where he had left plain cuttings of silk—there lay the most beautifullest coat and embroidered satin waistcoat that ever were worn by a Mayor of Gloucester.

Everything was finished except just one single cherry-coloured button-hole, and where that button-hole was wanting there was pinned a scrap of paper with these words—in little teeny weeny writing—

NO MORE TWIST

And from then on began the luck of the Tailor of Gloucester; he grew quite stout, and he grew quite rich.

He made the most wonderful waistcoats for all the rich merchants of Gloucester, and for all the fine gentlemen of the country round.

Never were seen such ruffles, or such embroidered cuffs and lappets! But his button-holes were the greatest triumph of it all.

The stitches of those button-holes were so neat—*so* neat—I wonder how they could be stitched by an old man in spectacles, with crooked old fingers, and a tailor's thimble.

The stitches of those button-holes were so small—*so* small—they looked as if they had been made by little mice!

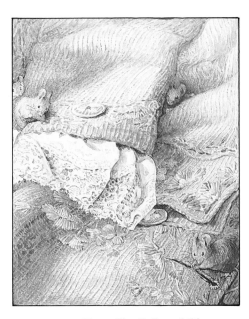

From *The Tailor of Gloucester*

37

Needle Work

Lavender Bag

For this project you will need a scrap of pretty material, pins, a needle and thread, and about 20 cm (8 in) of narrow ribbon.

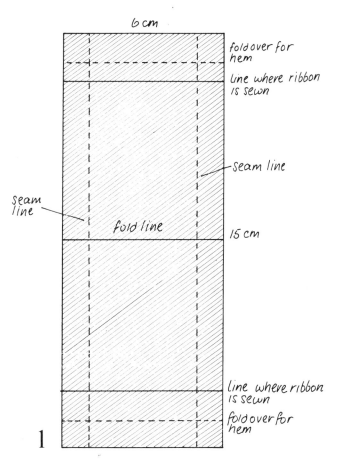

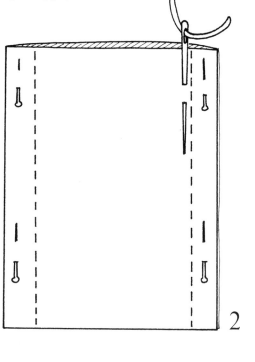

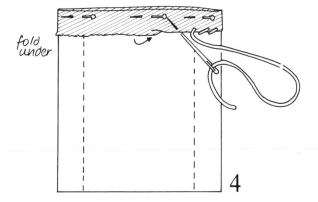

shaded areas show right side of fabric

Cut out of the material a piece 15 cm (6 in) long and 6 cm (2½ in) wide (diagram 1). Fold it across the centre widthways with the right sides of the material facing each other. Pin, then stitch a seam line 1 cm (½ in) from the edge along both sides (diagram 2). Remove the pins.

Fold the top 1 cm (½ in) over (diagram 3) and pin just below the fold line. Be careful not to pin both sides of the bag together. Fold the edge of the material under and stitch all the way round (diagram 4). Remove the pins.

Turn the bag the right way round, pressing the seams flat with your fingers. In line with the hem you have just stitched, sew about 1 cm (½ in) in the centre of the ribbon to the bag. Fill the bag with dried lavender flowers (see page 45) and tie the ribbon round the neck in a bow (diagram 5).

Lavender bags are easy to sew and make very attractive presents.

Sew-on Rabbit

For this project you will need some light brown felt and matching thread, some pale blue felt and matching thread, some dark brown embroidery thread, some white wool, pins and a needle. The rabbit can be sewn on to a sweater, a dressing-gown, a dress, a bag, a jacket, and so on.

First of all trace the rabbit pattern (diagram 1) off on to tracing paper. Lay the tracing paper over the brown felt and pin it in place, just inside the outline of the rabbit. Cut out the rabbit very carefully. Don't worry about his whiskers and tail for the time being.

Next take a tracing of the jacket pattern (diagram 2) and lay that over the blue felt. Pin it to the felt just inside the jacket's outline and cut the jacket out.

Decide where you want to position the rabbit on your garment and pin it in place, then stitch neatly round the edges using the matching brown thread.

Take another tracing off diagram 1 and place it over your rabbit, pinning it exactly over the top. Using the dark brown embroidery thread, sew in the eye and whiskers, as shown in

39

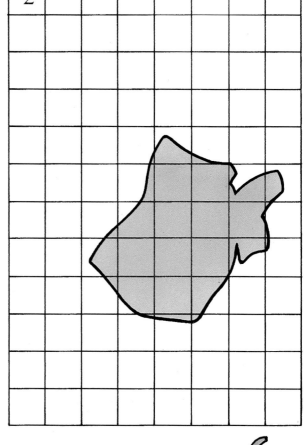

diagrams 3 and 4. This is done *over* the tracing paper, which can be gently removed later.

Position the jacket over the rabbit, matching the edges exactly, then sew it in place with the blue thread along the rabbit's back, neck and arms, but leaving the front below the arm and lower edges free.

To make the tail, cut out a piece of cardboard as shown in diagram 5. Lay a piece of white wool along the top of the card then wind the wool round the card. The more you wind the fluffier the tail will be. Tie the end of the wool to the end you left on top of the card, then cut the other ends carefully with scissors. Give the tail a shake to fluff it up then sew it in place on the rabbit.

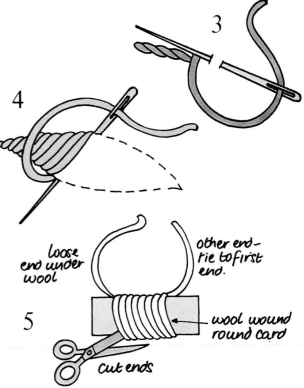

The Peter Rabbit Quiz

See how much you know about the Peter Rabbit characters in this book by trying to answer these twenty questions. Make sure you have read the book first, though! If you get really stuck, the answers are given on page 64.

1. Where did Jeremy Fisher live?
2. Who smoked rabbit-tobacco?
3. Which pig ate peppermints?

4. What were Tom Kitten's sisters called?
5. Who was Old Brown?
6. Who wanted to hatch her own eggs?
7. Ginger was a dog and Pickles a cat. True or false?
8. Mrs Tittlemouse was very untidy. True or false?
9. How many Flopsy Bunnies were there?

10. Why was a skein of cherry-coloured twist needed by some workers in Gloucester?
11. Who offered Jeremy Fisher a snail for dinner?
12. What relation was Benjamin Bunny to Peter Rabbit?
13. Who scratched a cat?
14. Whose brother was Twinkle-berry?

15. How did Mrs. Tiggy-winkle earn her living?
16. Who couldn't eat his dinner for lack of teeth?
17. What had happened to Peter Rabbit's father?
18. Whose pet was Simpkin?
19. Who met Nanny Nettigoat?
20. Where did the *real* Peter Rabbit live?

What's in a Name?

These funny animals are all made up from the letters of their names. Can you work out what each one is?

A Cat Tale

Peter Rabbit and his cousin Benjamin were taking onions from Mr. McGregor's garden. Peter was uneasy and kept hearing strange noises. He peeped round a corner, and....

This is what those little rabbits saw round that corner!

Little Benjamin took one look, and then, in half a minute less than no time, he hid himself and Peter and the onions underneath a large basket....

The cat got up and stretched herself, and came and sniffed at the basket.

Perhaps she liked the smell of onions!

Anyway, she sat down upon the top of the basket.

She sat there for *five hours.*

Meanwhile old Mr. Benjamin Bunny came looking for his son.

Old Mr. Bunny had no opinion whatever of cats.

He took a tremendous jump off the top of the wall on to the top of the cat, and cuffed it off the basket, and kicked it into the green-house, scratching off a handful of fur.

The cat was too much surprised to scratch back.

43

From *The Tale of Benjamin Bunny*

"Rabbit-Tobacco"

Old Mrs. Rabbit, the mother of Peter, Flopsy, Mopsy and Cotton-tail, and the aunt of young Benjamin, sold rabbit-tobacco, which is what *we* call lavender.

Old Mr. Benjamin Bunny (young Benjamin's father) used to smoke the rabbit-tobacco in his pipe.

We grow and harvest lavender for its sweet-smelling flowers, which can be dried and put in little bags in drawers to make clothes smell nice.

Lavender grows best in a sunny spot in rather stony soil. You can grow it in the garden or in a pot outside, and the easiest and cheapest way to grow it is to take cuttings from a friend's plant. This is what you do.

Put a layer of gravel in the bottom of a 10-cm (4-in) flowerpot, then fill it with a mixture of earth and sand. Water it until all the soil is damp and water drains out of the bottom.

Break off some shoots that don't have flowers on them that are about 12 cm (5 in) long from the parent plant, leaving a "heel" (diagram 1). Pull the leaves off the bottom halves of the cuttings, and push the stems into the soil round the edge of the pot (diagram 2). Water the cuttings when the soil dries out, and when they start to grow new leaves, plant them out in the garden or carefully lift them out of

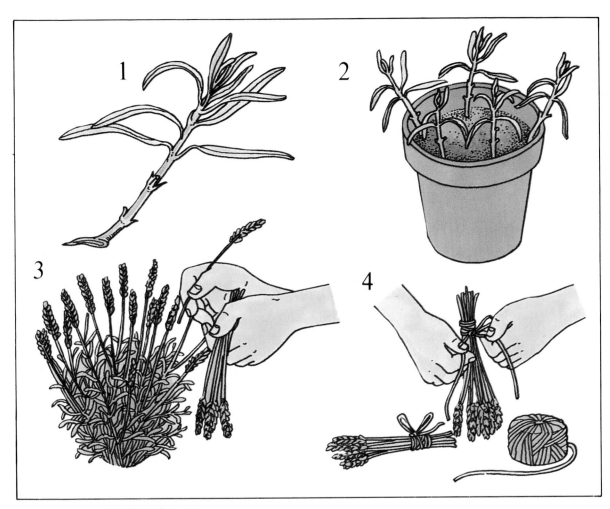

their pot and put them in a bigger one, with fresh soil. Handle them very carefully so you don't damage the tiny new roots.

The best time to harvest the flowers is on a warm, sunny day. Break off whole stems about 20 to 25 cm long (8 to 9 in) (diagram 3), tie them together in small bunches (diagram 4), and hang them up in a dry and well-ventilated place, such as a spare bedroom, to dry out until the flowers can be rubbed off the stems. They can then be used to fill little bags (see page 38) or kept in a bowl to perfume a room.

How to Make a Pop-up Card

Here's how to make your very own pop-up card. The pictures are taken from *The Tale of Mrs. Tiggy-Winkle*. The front of the card shows Lucie looking for her lost handkerchiefs and pinafore, and the inside shows Mrs. Tiggy-winkle busy with her washing and ironing.

You will need
1 piece of card 16cm (6in) wide x 10cm (4in) deep
2 pieces of card 14cm (5½in) wide x 8cm (3in) deep
a pencil
a ruler
a pair of scissors
some paste
paints or crayons for colouring
tracing paper

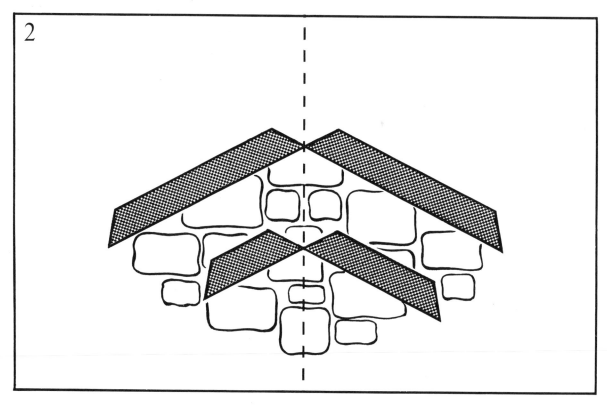

46

1. Draw a light pencil line down the centre of the larger piece of card. Score along it using the blunt tips of the scissors but do not cut.

2. Trace off the floor pattern and diagonal shaded areas from diagram 2. These areas mark where the flaps on the pictures of Mrs. Tiggy-winkle and her kitchen are stuck.

3. Fold the card down the scored line. On its front trace off the picture of Lucie (diagram 1) and colour it in.

4. On one of the smaller pieces of card trace off the drawing of Mrs. Tiggy-winkle (diagram 3). Don't forget the two little flaps. Lightly mark a line down the centre of the picture then cut it out, including the flaps.

5. On the second smaller piece of card trace off the drawing of Mrs. Tiggy-winkle's kitchen, again remembering the flaps (diagram 4). Mark the centre of the picture then cut it out too.

6. Colour in your two pictures.

7. Fold the pictures in half down the marked lines and fold the flaps back. Put some paste on the flaps.

8. Stick the kitchen picture in line with the upper marks across the larger piece of card, and the Mrs. Tiggy-winkle picture in line with the lower ones. Leave the card until the paste is dry.

9. Fold the pictures carefully and close the card. When you open it again the pictures should spring into life!

10. You can make your pop-up card into a birthday card, a thank-you card, or whatever you like by writing a suitable message on the back.

Nature Notebook

Whether you live in the country or the town you can enjoy studying animals, birds and plants. Beatrix Potter made notes in her journal about the birds, animals, trees and flowers she saw both when she was in London and on her stays in the country. Why not follow her example and keep a nature notebook?

Your studies may take place in your garden, in local parks, on patches of waste ground, in the country—you could even observe plants and insects on a windowsill! Wherever you are, remember that if you want to watch wild creatures you must learn to keep still and quiet. In your notebook write down the date and time, the weather, and the things you see. A typical entry might look like this:

> Saturday 22nd March
> In the garden   2:30 p.m.
> Leaf buds on trees swelling,
> most daffodils now out...
> sparrows carrying twigs
> for nest building,
> Saw blackbird pulling
> worm out of the ground..

It is also fun to carry out nature projects and record their progress in your notebook, too. Here are four to try—one for each season of the year.

Spring

In early spring the pussy-willow catkins open. Willow trees like moist ground, but pussy-willows may be found in places other than the edges of streams and lakes, unlike the weeping willow trees. Pussy-willow catkins are silver-grey when they open and feel soft and silky, but after a week or two they will become covered in yellow pollen and the tree will be full of bees on sunny days.

Collect a few twigs of pussy-willow, take them home, and put them in a vase of water. Keep the water topped up and the ends of the twigs will start to grow roots. They can then be planted in the garden to grow a willow tree of your own.

Summer

Grey squirrels are very common in gardens and parks and great fun to watch as they run and leap gracefully from branch to branch. If they are fed regularly they become very tame. Try putting out nuts at a regular time each day and your squirrel will come and eat them. Gradually get it used to seeing you with the nuts, and one day hold one out in your hand and if you are lucky the squirrel will learn to eat from your hand. Note in your book how long it takes you to tame the squirrel, and how it behaves.

Autumn

Autumn is the time to look out for spiders. In the early mornings you will see their webs glistening with dew-drops in the hedgerows. If you watch carefully you may see a spider spinning its web. First of all it builds

the outside frame, then the radial threads, then it connects these with a spiral to support them. Finally it spins a sticky thread with which it catches its prey. A kind of trip wire tells the spider when it has caught an insect.

See how many different kinds of webs and spiders you can find, and note what they have caught to eat. Draw a web in your notebook,

labelling the framework, the radial threads and the supporting spiral.

Winter

In winter put out food for the birds and you can help to keep them alive through the cold weather and enjoy watching them at the same time. They will enjoy bacon rinds, moistened bread, cake, pastry, nuts (not salted), fruit, cheese, cooked rice, cat or dog food, and the special seed mixtures sold at pet shops. Try and put the food out of reach of cats, or they may pounce on the birds. If you hang up nuts on threads, and smear fat on the bark of a tree, you will have fun watching the antics of the birds as they eat. Put out water for birds too, for many die of thirst in freezing weather. When the water freezes over, replace it with warm water. A large plant saucer makes a good bird trough, and they will enjoy bathing in it too, even on cold days. Note down which birds you see at which times, which foods they seem to prefer, and their behaviour towards other birds.

Baking Day

Here's how to make some delicious things to eat for a party, or just to enjoy at any time.

Gingerbread Animals

To make these you will need some animal-shaped cutters, but if you don't have any you can make them as ordinary round ginger cookies, which will taste just as good.

Ingredients
(to make 24 animals/shapes)
100g (1 cup) plain flour
1 level teaspoon baking powder
1 level teaspoon bicarbonate of
    soda (baking soda)
1 - 2 level teaspoons ground ginger
1 level teaspoon ground cinnamon
50g (¼ cup) sugar
50g (¼ cup) butter or margarine
3 tablespoons golden syrup
currants

1. Ask an adult to set the oven at 190°C, 375°F, Gas Mark 5.
2. Brush two baking sheets with oil.
3. Into a mixing bowl sieve together the flour, baking powder, bicarbonate of soda (baking soda), ginger, cinnamon and sugar.
4. Melt the butter or margarine, and mix it with the golden syrup.
5. Stir the butter/margarine and syrup mixture into the dry ingredients. Mix together well.
6. Sprinkle the worktop and a rolling-pin with flour.
7. Roll the mixture into a ball with your hands and put it on the floured worktop. Roll it out flat with the rolling-pin until it is about 3mm (¼in) thick.

8. Cut out the shapes with the animal cutters or make them into rounds.

9. Gather up the left-over pieces, roll them into a ball, then roll them out flat and cut out more shapes. Do this until all the mixture has been used.

10. Put a currant on each shape for the eye.

11. Put the animals on the greased baking sheets and bake in the centre of the oven for about 15 - 20 minutes.

12. Ask an adult to get them out of the oven for you, and put them to cool on a wire rack.

Chocolate Crispies
(to make 12)

Ingredients
100g (4 oz) plain chocolate
50g (1 cup) cornflakes or rice crispies
25g (2 tablespoons) butter or margarine

1. Break the chocolate into pieces in a bowl and add the butter or margarine.

2. Sit the bowl in a saucepan of hot water. Put the pan over a low heat on the stove.

3. Stir the mixture until it has melted and run together.

4. Ask an adult to lift the bowl out of the pan for you. It may be quite hot so be careful not to touch it.

5. Mix in the cornflakes or rice crispies.

6. Spoon the mixture out into waxed paper cases or on to a baking sheet and leave until cool.

Squirrel Nutkin's Riddles

Squirrel Nutkin lived with his brother Twinkleberry and a great many cousins in a wood at the edge of a lake. One autumn the squirrels sailed across the lake to Owl Island in its centre to gather nuts. The island was owned by a large owl called Old Brown and the squirrels were a bit afraid of him and very polite—all except Squirrel Nutkin, who was an impertinent young animal. He danced up and down in front of Old Brown, teasing him and asking him riddles.

Here are some of Squirrel Nutkin's riddles. Can you guess the answers? In the story they are given in the text; in this book they are given on page 64, but don't look until you have tried to solve them.

1

Riddle me, riddle me, rot-tot-tote!
A little wee man, in a red red coat!
A staff in his hand, and a stone in his
  throat;
If you'll tell me this riddle, I'll give
  you a groat.

Clue: a fruit we eat, and make into jam.

2

Old Mr. B! Riddle-me-ree!
Hitty Pitty within the wall,
Hitty Pitty without the wall;
If you touch Hitty Pitty,
Hitty Pitty will bite you!

Clue: a plant that stings.

3

Old Mr. B! Riddle-me-ree!
Flour of England, fruit of Spain,
Met together in a shower of rain;
Put in a bag tied round with a string,
If you'll tell me this riddle, I'll give
    you a ring!

Clue: something eaten at Christmas-time.

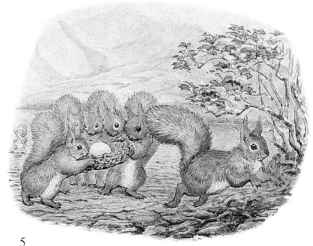

5

Humpty Dumpty lies in the beck,
With a white counterpane round his
    neck,
Forty doctors and forty wrights,
Cannot put Humpty Dumpty to
    rights!

4

Hum-a-bum! buzz! buzz! Hum-a-bum
    buzz!
As I went over Tipple-tine
I met a flock of bonny swine;
Some yellow-nacked, some yellow
    backed!
They were the very bonniest swine
That e'er went over Tipple-tine.

Clue: insects that make honey.

6

Old Mr. B! Old Mr. B!
Hickamore, Hackamore, on the
    King's kitchen door;
All the King's horses, and all the
    King's men,
Couldn't drive Hickamore,
    Hackamore,
Off the King's kitchen door.

Clue: a ray of light.

From *The Tale of Squirrel Nutkin*

Three Naughty Kittens

Mrs. Tabitha Twitchit expected friends to tea; so she fetched the kittens indoors, to wash and dress them, before the fine company arrived.

She dressed Moppet and Mittens in clean pinafores and tuckers; and then she took all sorts of elegant uncomfortable clothes out of a chest of drawers, in order to dress up her son Thomas.

Tom Kitten was very fat, and he had grown; several buttons burst off. His mother sewed them on again.

When the three kittens were ready, Mrs. Tabitha unwisely turned them out into the garden, to be out of the way while she made hot buttered toast.

"Now keep your frocks clean, children! You must walk on your hind legs. Keep away from the dirty ashpit, and from Sally Henny Penny, and from the pig-stye and the Puddle-ducks."

From *The Tale of Tom Kitten*

But the three kittens didn't keep their clothes clean at all! Tom burst his buttons so his suit fell off, and Moppet and Mittens dropped their pinafores and tuckers. When they got home their mother was so cross she sent them straight to bed. The two large pictures show what they did when they were supposed to be in bed!

These pictures show the same scene but they are not exactly alike. See how many differences you can spot between them. You should be able to find ten.

Peter Rabbit's Almanac

JANUARY

1	2	3	4	5	6	7
8	9	10	11	12	13	14
15	16	17	18	19	20	21
22	23	24	25	26	27	28
29	30	31				

Special Days
1st New Year's Day

FEBRUARY

1	2	3	4	5	6	7
8	9	10	11	12	13	14
15	16	17	18	19	20	21
22	23	24	25	26	27	28
29						

Special Days
14th St. Valentine's Day

MAY

1	2	3	4	5	6	7
8	9	10	11	12	13	14
15	16	17	18	19	20	21
22	23	24	25	26	27	28
29	30	31				

Special Days
1st May Day

JUNE

1	2	3	4	5	6	7
8	9	10	11	12	13	14
15	16	17	18	19	20	21
22	23	24	25	26	27	28
29	30					

Special Days
24th Midsummer Day

SEPTEMBER

1	2	3	4	5	6	7
8	9	10	11	12	13	14
15	16	17	18	19	20	21
22	23	24	25	26	27	28
29	30					

Special Days

OCTOBER

1	2	3	4	5	6	7
8	9	10	11	12	13	14
15	16	17	18	19	20	21
22	23	24	25	26	27	28
29	30	31				

Special Days
31st Hallowe'en

This calendar can be used any year, and each month has a space for you to fill in special days, such as friends' birthdays, ends of terms and family holidays.

MARCH	
1 2 3 4 5 6 7	
8 9 10 11 12 13 14	
15 16 17 18 19 20 21	
22 23 24 25 26 27 28	
29 30 31	
Special Days	
21st The first day of spring	

APRIL	
1 2 3 4 5 6 7	
8 9 10 11 12 13 14	
15 16 17 18 19 20 21	
22 23 24 25 26 27 28	
29 30	
Special Days	
1st All Fools' Day	

JULY	
1 2 3 4 5 6 7	
8 9 10 11 12 13 14	
15 16 17 18 19 20 21	
22 23 24 25 26 27 28	
29 30 31	
Special Days	
28th Beatrix Potter's birthday	

AUGUST	
1 2 3 4 5 6 7	
8 9 10 11 12 13 14	
15 16 17 18 19 20 21	
22 23 24 25 26 27 28	
29 30 31	
Special Days	

NOVEMBER	
1 2 3 4 5 6 7	
8 9 10 11 12 13 14	
15 16 17 18 19 20 21	
22 23 24 25 26 27 28	
29 30	
Special Days	
5th Guy Fawkes Day (UK)	

DECEMBER	
1 2 3 4 5 6 7	
8 9 10 11 12 13 14	
15 16 17 18 19 20 21	
22 23 24 25 26 27 28	
29 30 31	
Special Days	
25th Christmas Day	

How to Give a Party

It is always fun to have a party, whether it is to celebrate your birthday, Christmas, Hallowe'en, or any other time. The best parties have a theme, and on these pages you'll find some ideas for a Peter Rabbit party.

Of course your mother or father have to help you organise a party but it is much more fun if you do a lot of it yourself. The first thing is to decide when the party will be held. If it is to be a birthday party and your birthday is on a week-day, you may prefer to have the party on a Saturday or a Sunday when there is more time to get things ready. It all depends on what is convenient for the family.

When you have chosen the date make a guest list and send out your invitations. Do this about a month before the party to make sure that everyone will be able to come. Page 30 shows you how to write an invitation.

Food and Drink

When you know how many people are coming you can plan the food. For a summer party you'll want sandwiches, ice-cream, jelly and cold drinks, but for a winter party hot food would be better, such as jacket potatoes, sausages and mugs of soup or cocoa. Pages 50 and 51 show you how to make gingerbread animals and chocolate crispies, both of which are good party food. Here are some recipes for Peter Rabbit party food.

Jeremy Fisher's Butterfly Sandwiches

Ingredients (to make 8)
4 slices of brown bread
4 slices of white bread
cream cheese
some of the following: small carrots, radishes, cucumber, dates, slices of cooked ham, sticks of celery.

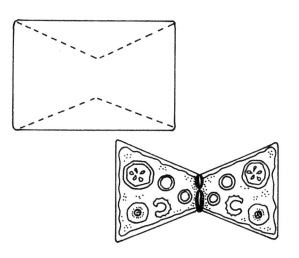

1. Remove the crusts from the bread.
2. Cut out two triangles from each slice as shown.
3. Spread the bread with cream cheese. On the brown bread, leave a border of brown showing round the edge.
4. Make the butterfly bodies out of the dates, chopped up celery sticks or rolled slices of ham. Lay them down the centre.

5. Make wing decorations from thin slices of carrot, radish or cucumber. The decorations on both wings should match.

6. Use the left-over triangles to make small covered sandwiches with the same fillings and serve them on a separate plate.

As well as delicious food you will need a choice of drinks. You can have lemonade, orangeade, ginger beer, coke and milk shakes, but for something really special, make a fruit punch. It can be served chilled, with ice cubes, in summer, or hot in winter.

Mrs. Tittlemouse's Fruit Punch

Ingredients
1 litre of orange juice
1 litre of apple juice
1 litre of pineapple juice
some cloves and sugar, if serving hot
a small apple
an orange

1. To serve the punch cold, simply mix all the fruit juices together in a big bowl.

2. Wash the apple and the orange and slice them thinly. Float the slices on the surface of the punch.

3. To serve the punch hot, put the fruit juices in a pan with 3 tablespoons of sugar and a few cloves. Put the pan on a burner on the stove to heat through, and stir the juices until the sugar has melted. Do not let the juices boil.

4. When the punch is hot, pour it carefully into a warmed bowl and float the fruit slices on the top as before.

Decorations

You will want the room in which the party is being held to look pretty. Ask an adult to help you hang up coloured streamers, and to blow up balloons and tie them in bunches to hang up, too. If it is Christmas time you may have bunches of holly and mistletoe in the house. You can also make place cards for the table, like the ones Beatrix Potter made.

Two of Beatrix Potter's place cards

Games

You will also need to plan in advance some games to play. You probably have favourites of your own, but here are some special Peter Rabbit games.

Peppermint Party Talk

If you have made the peppermints on page 26 you may have wondered why they have letters on them. It is for this game! But before you can play it, you also need to make some little labels to pin on your guests. The labels go in pairs, each half of the pair having the name of a Peter Rabbit character on it which links together with another Peter Rabbit character. For example, you might have Ginger and Pickles, Moppet and Mittens, Flopsy and Mopsy, Samuel Whiskers and Anna Maria. You will find a complete list of pair names on page 64 and you should write this out so that anyone who

Pig-wig eating peppermints

doesn't know his or her character's partner can look it up.

As each of your guests arrives, offer them a peppermint and pin one of the name labels on them. Have the labels ready but mixed up, so the next person doesn't necessarily get the other half of the pair. Each guest then has to seek out his or her partner, look at the letter on the peppermint, and try to talk to the partner for five minutes using as many words beginning with the letter on the peppermint as they can. The partner with the larger number of words wins both mints!

Mr. McGregor's Garden

To play this game you need at least six players and a number of large handkerchiefs or scarves to act as blindfolds.

One player is chosen to be Peter Rabbit and stands in the middle of the room. The other players are the fence around Mr. McGregor's garden and they stand round Peter leaving *just enough* room for him to walk between them. These 'fence' players should be blindfolded, but if you haven't got enough blindfolds then they must keep their eyes tightly closed.

Once the 'fence' players are ready, Peter must say, 'I'm Peter Rabbit and I'm going to escape from Mr. McGregor's garden,' and he must tip-toe out of the circle. If any of the 'fence' players thinks they can hear Peter escaping, they must point at him. If someone points in the right direction, then that player changes places with Peter and becomes the new Peter for the next round.

Squirrel Nutkin's Tail

If you have read *The Tale of Squirrel Nutkin* you will know that he lost his tail because he was cheeky once too often to Old Brown the owl. Here's a chance to give Nutkin back his tail. You will need a large drawing of him, a separate drawing of his tail, a pinboard or blackboard, a drawing-pin, and a blindfold.

The drawing of Nutkin is fixed to the pinboard or blackboard and the drawing-pin is pushed through the top of the tail ready to fix it in place. Then one by one the players are blindfolded, led to the drawing, and told to pin the tail on Squirrel Nutkin. Those watching will have as much fun as the player whose turn it is, as they watch him pin the tail in Nutkin's ear, or on his nose! After each player has had a turn, mark where he or she put the tail and initial it, so that at the end you can see who got the nearest to the right place. This player is the winner.

Mrs. Tittlemouse's party

For some games you may need prizes. Pages 26 and 27 described how to make sweets, and these would make very good prizes if wrapped up nicely in pretty paper.

Sweets would also make good going home presents, or you could make and wrap up some gingerbread animals (page 50) or lavender bags (page 38) and give these to your friends instead.

Squirrel Nutkin (on the left) after Old Brown had pulled off half his tail

 # Peter Rabbit's Party

You can have all your favourite Peter Rabbit characters at your party if you trace the figures below and opposite on to thin card and cut them out. Colour them with crayons or water-colour paints, then fold back the tabs at the bottom of each to stand them up. Open the book at the inside front or back cover and stand it behind the characters to provide the right background.

Answers to Puzzles

Code Writing *page 15*

Beatrix Potter had a tame rabbit called Peter.
Peter's cousin Benjamin married Flopsy, Peter's sister.
Peter was a naughty rabbit who disobeyed his mother.

A Puddle-Duck's Puzzle *page 23*

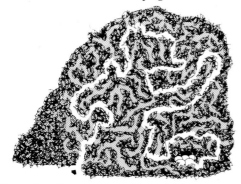

Shopping Spree *pages 28 and 29*

Page 28
1. Taking nuts from the sack by the door.
2. Chicks and ducklings.
3. Blue.
4. A tortoise (probably Mr. Ptolemy Tortoise).
5. The names 'Ginger & Pickles' written over the shop window.

Page 29
1. Four.
2. A rat (probably Mr. Samuel Whiskers).
3. Ginger.
4. The frog (Mr. Jeremy Fisher).
5. Peter Rabbit (the rabbit in the blue jacket).
6. Two – Ginger and the rat.
7. Three – the rabbits, apart from Peter.

The Peter Rabbit Quiz *page 41*

1. In a little damp house amongst the buttercups at the edge of a pond (page 24).
2. Old Mr. Benjamin Bunny (page 44).
3. Pig-wig (page 60).
4. Moppet and Mittens (page 54).
5. The owl who owned the island where Squirrel Nutkin and his friends and relations went to gather nuts (page 52).
6. Jemima Puddle-duck (page 20).
7. False. It was the other way round (page 28).
8. False (page 31).
9. Six (page 5).

10. To finish the last button-hole on the Mayor's coat (page 34).
11. Mr. Alderman Ptolemy Tortoise (page 30).
12. His cousin (page 5).
13. Old Mr. Benjamin Bunny (page 43).
14. Squirrel Nutkin's (page 52).
15. She was a washerwoman (page 46).
16. Mr. Jackson, the toad (page 33).
17. He had been put in a pie by Mrs. McGregor (page 5).
18. The tailor of Gloucester's (page 34).
19. Little Pig Robinson (page 18).
20. At Beatrix Potter's house in London (page 6).

What's in a Name? *page 42*
1. Rabbit.   3. Hedgehog.
2. Squirrel.   4. Mouse.

Squirrel Nutkin's Riddles *page 52*
1. A cherry.   4. Bees.
2. A nettle.   5. An egg.
3. A plum-pudding.   6. A sunbeam.

Three Naughty Kittens *page 54*

List of Pairs for Peppermint Party Talk *page 60*

Peter Rabbit and Benjamin Bunny
Flopsy and Mopsy
Moppet and Mittens
Jemima Puddle-duck and Mr. Drake Puddle-duck
Ribby and Duchess
Pigling Bland and Pig-wig
Ginger and Pickles
Samuel Whiskers and Anna Maria
Hunca Munca and Tom Thumb
Mr. Tod and Tommy Brock
Timmy Tiptoes and Goody Tiptoes
Johnny Town-mouse and Timmy Willie